It's Easter, Chloe Zoe!

Jane Smith

Albert Whitman & Company
Chicago, Illinois

It's Easter!

Easter is a springtime celebration.

I help my daddy plant new flowers in our garden.

We decorate our house with pretty baskets and fuzzy bunnies.

I dye eggs a rainbow of colors with my mommy and little sister.

Today is the big Easter egg hunt! Every year the Easter Bunny hides hundreds of pretty painted eggs and toys and candy all over the park.

He also hides one special, sparkling golden egg with a surprise inside. No one knows what the surprise will be! This year, I'm going to find it!

On the walk over to the park, we see George and his family. "Hi, George," I say.

“I’m going to find *so* much candy,” George says.
“I’m going to find the golden egg,” I say.

At the park, Mary Margaret runs up to us with a fancy Easter basket.

“Chloe Zoe is going to find the golden egg,” says George.

“Yay! I’m going to find all the pink eggs!” says Mary Margaret.

Everyone gathers together by the big fountain to begin the Easter egg hunt. The mayor hushes the crowd and counts, "One, two, three, GO!" Everyone runs!

I find a yellow-polka-dot egg and a pink-striped egg in some flowers.

George finds three chocolate bunnies high up in a tree.

Everyone's Easter baskets are filling up. Everyone's except Mary Margaret's.

“You haven’t found any eggs yet?” I ask her.

“I only want the pink ones,” she says, “and they are really well hidden!” Mary Margaret’s favorite color is pink.

I hand Mary Margaret the pink-striped egg I found earlier. "Don't worry! I'll find more for you, Mary Margaret!"

"Me too!" says George.

After all, I think, *there's still plenty of time to find the golden egg.*

We all look for pink eggs. Every place I look for pink eggs, I check for the golden egg too.

George finds one egg filled with jelly beans next to a bird's nest. And I find two eggs under a big mushroom. Then I hear Mary Margaret's voice.

"Ooh! I found the Golden Egg!"

"Chloe Zoe! George! Come look!"

I feel my cheeks get hot. I run to my mommy.

"I'm sorry, Chloe Zoe. I know how much you wanted to find the golden egg yourself," my mommy says. "But look at all the goodies you did find—eggs, toys, and candy!"

"I *am* having a lot of fun, especially finding pink eggs for Mary Margaret…"

Just then, Mary Margaret runs over with George. "We couldn't open the golden egg without you!" says Mary Margaret.

Mary Margaret cracks open the golden egg. Inside are three sparkling gold coins!

"Perfect!" squeals Mary Margaret as she hands a coin each to George and me. "Three coins for three best friends!"

"Happy Easter, everyone!" I cheer.

"Happy Easter, Chloe Zoe!" George and Mary Margaret say.

For more Chloe Zoe fun
—like crafts, coloring pages, games, and activities—
visit www.albertwhitman.com.

For Phoebe Love—my favorite studio buddy

Also available:
It's Valentine's Day, Chloe Zoe!

More Chloe Zoe books coming soon:
It's the First Day of Preschool, Chloe Zoe!
It's the First Day of Kindergarten, Chloe Zoe!

Library of Congress Cataloging-in-Publication data is on file with the publisher.

Published in 2016 by Albert Whitman & Company
ISBN 978-0-8075-2460-2

Printed in China
10 9 8 7 6 5 4 3 2 1 HH 24 23 22 21 20 19 18 17 16 15

Design by Jordan Kost

For more information about Albert Whitman & Company, visit our web site at www.albertwhitman.com.